SWIFTY

The Magic Aeroplane

(Book 1)

By

David Lindsey

Shield Crest

ISBN: 978-1-913839-58-1

MMXXII

A CIP catalogue record for this
is available from the British Library

Published by
ShieldCrest Publishing,
Bicker, Lincs, PE20 3BT England
Tel: +44 (0) 333 8000 890
www.shieldcrest.co.uk

This book is dedicated to my dear wife, who steadfastly supported me through many lonely hours spent waiting for me to finish my day's work writing at my laptop.

Contents

1
How It All Began

I expect you would like to know how Jimmy met Swifty. Well, I'll tell you.

Jimmy Robinson loved to go to the airfield when he was a small boy. He liked to watch the aeroplanes taking off and landing, and the people getting in to fly to other towns and countries. He thought it was very exciting.

The little boy also liked to go into the hangar and watch the men working on the aeroplanes which had something wrong with them. Jimmy's daddy was in charge of the men in the hangar and that is why Jimmy was allowed to go into the huge building.

One day he was wandering around the hangar while the men were having their lunch when he heard the sound of crying. He couldn't see where it was coming from so he searched and searched and eventually he found that the noise was coming from a large piece of canvas draped in the far corner of the hangar.

Jimmy tugged and tugged at the canvas until it finally came away and there, in the corner, was a dirty little aeroplane. It was covered with splodges of oil; the tyres were flat and it had no propeller.

"Oh, please won't somebody mend me, I do so want to fly again!" said the sad little voice, and Jimmy couldn't believe his ears.

Aeroplanes don't talk, he thought. *Somebody is playing a trick on me.*

But there was no one else in the hangar.

"Will you help me, little boy?" said the voice, "Nobody wants me any more because they think I am too old, but with a new coat of paint, some air in my tyres, petrol in my tank and a new propeller, I shall be as good as new again, and I am a magic aeroplane."

Jimmy was so excited that he went round to the control tower and asked Mr Satco the Airport Manager if anyone owned the little aeroplane. The man said "No," so Jimmy asked if he could have it to play with.

"Yes, of course you can, Jimmy," replied the kind man. "It will keep you out of mischief," he added with a smile.

Jimmy said thank you and went back to the hangar to tell the little aeroplane the news.

"My name is Jimmy, and you belong to me now," said the little boy.

"Well, my name is Swifty," replied the aeroplane, "and I am very pleased to meet you. If you can mend me, I shall show you how to fly me and we shall be able to go all sorts of places together."

Jimmy and Swifty decided to keep it a secret that the aeroplane was being mended so Jimmy only worked on Swifty when the men were away and before they returned Jimmy would put the cover back over the little machine so that the men couldn't see how much better Swifty was beginning to look.

Jimmy had set to work with soap and rags, and then with yellow and silver paint that he found in the corner, and in a week or two, the little aeroplane sparkled and shone.

He got the pump from his red car and pumped up the tyres and then all he needed was a propeller. He went back to see Mr Satco, who was in charge of the control tower.

"Please sir, have you got a propeller that nobody wants?" he asked.

"Well, the only one I've got is the one which came off that dirty little thing you play with in the hangar, Jimmy," replied the man. "It is too small for any of the other machines, so you can have that one with pleasure."

Jimmy was overjoyed. He used some equipment from the hangar to hoist up and fit the propeller and a week later, just as Swifty had promised, the little aeroplane looked like new.

The next day, while the men were having their lunch, Jimmy poured some petrol into Swifty's tank and climbed into the cabin.

"Well, Swifty, we are ready to go, but I don't know how to fly an aeroplane."

"Don't you worry about that, Jimmy," replied the little machine, "I told you that I am a magic aeroplane. Just press that little green starter button and leave the rest to me. I'll teach you how to fly."

And that's exactly what he did.

The workmen were astonished when they heard a roar and a beautiful little aeroplane zoomed out of the hangar with Jimmy sitting in the cockpit. At first, they were so astonished that they couldn't move, and then they were frightened that the little boy would crash and hurt himself, but when they saw the aeroplane dancing through the sky, doing perfect loops and turns and finally a perfect landing, they just stood and cheered.

One man who was standing watching asked Jimmy if he could buy the little aeroplane, but Jimmy said that he would never part with his lovely little machine, and he never, never did.

2

The Redville Airlift

Jimmy was sitting at home one day in the winter, watching the snow come down like feathers outside the window. Jimmy liked the winter. He loved looking at the patterns that Mummy said Jack Frost had made on the window during the night.

He was just about to put on his warm clothes so that he could go and ride on his sledge with little Johnny Green when the telephone rang.

It was Mr Satco from the airfield. "Good morning Jimmy," he said. "I wonder if you can help me? We have had a telephone call from Mrs Merry to say that the snow is so deep at the farm that she can't get into Redville to do her shopping and she is running out of food. Mr Barley the miller lives just down the road from Mrs Merry so he is probably running short of food too. We won't be able to clear the road to them for a few days yet, so we are worried about them. Do you think that you and Swifty could help us?"

"Well if you can provide some parachutes for me to drop the food to them from Swifty's cabin, I shall be glad to help," replied Jimmy.

"I'm sure we have some somewhere," said Mr Satco. "You ring up Mrs Merry to ask her what she wants, and I'll sort out the parachutes."

Jimmy replaced the telephone then picked it up again to ring Mrs Merry.

"Hello," he called. "Is that you, Mrs Merry? I hear that you can't get into Redville and that you are running short of food. Swifty and I are going to fly over to Cherry Tree Farm and drop some things down to you by parachute, so would you like to tell me the things you need?"

"Well, you *are* a good boy," said the farmer's wife. "Here is a list of the things we would like to have."

Jimmy got his paper and pencil out.

"I would like some meat, some flour to make the bread, some jam, some tins of baked beans, some sugar, some potatoes, some candles in case we get cut off from the electricity and six boxes of matches. Oh, and some tea. We have plenty of milk from our cows and eggs from the chickens."

Jimmy copied everything down on his piece of paper.

"Well, don't you worry Mrs Merry," he said, "Swifty and I will soon have the groceries delivered to you."

Then Jimmy rang Mr Barley and got a list of the things that the jolly miller required, then he went round to the garage and got out his red motor car. Twenty minutes later, with the back of the car loaded with parcels, he set off for the airfield. He had to drive quite slowly because there was a lot of ice on the road, but he got there quite safely and Mr Satco was waiting there for him.

"Hello Jimmy," he called. "I've found some parachutes and some sacks to put the food in, so let's get cracking."

In no time at all they had put the groceries into the sacks and attached the parachutes. The runway had been cleared of snow so Jimmy, Mr Satco and Swifty were soon racing into the air.

The countryside looked beautiful with its covering of snow, and it wasn't long before Mr Satco was pointing out the figure of Mrs Merry standing in the snow outside the farmhouse. They circled over the top of the house and then Jimmy called to Mr Satco, "Is the parachute ready?"

"Yes," he replied, "I am ready for the drop."

"Here we go then," said Jimmy. "I am flying towards the farmhouse now. Ready—ready…ready—*go!*" and Mr Satco pushed the bundle out.

They circled round, watching the parachute float gently down to land right at Mrs Merry's feet. A parachute is like a huge umbrella and when it opens, it allows people and things to float down gently to the ground

"Oh, good shot Jimmy," said Mr Satco, and with a wave to Mrs Merry, they were off in the direction of Mr Barley's mill.

Once again they managed to drop the parcel right at the feet of the miller then, after flying low over the mill, they set course back to the airfield.

When they got back both Mrs Merry and the miller rang up to say how grateful they were for having the food delivered and they said that they would be sending a special Christmas present to Jimmy because he had been such a good boy.

I wonder what they sent him?

3
Into the Mountains

Jimmy was sitting at home one day listening to the radio when the man who reads the news made a special announcement.

"Some Boy Scouts who were going to climb to the top of Blue Mountain cannot get back down because there has been a heavy fall of snow. They are nice and warm in their tent and they have plenty of food to last them for three days, but they have to go to school tomorrow, so we would like someone to climb up the mountain to rescue them."

Oh dear, thought Jimmy, *that will be a pity if they can't go to school tomorrow because we are all going to have our Christmas party in the afternoon.*

He sat down and began to read his book, which was about people who lived in a country which had a lot of high mountains and was called Switzerland. Jimmy turned over the page and on the next page was a picture. In the picture was an aeroplane but instead of wheels it had two long pieces of wood which were called skis and these allowed the aeroplane to land on the snow high up in the mountains of that country.

That gives me an idea, thought Jimmy. *I wonder if I could put some skis underneath Swifty's wheels and go up on to Blue Mountain to rescue those Boy Scouts.*

He went outside and got into his red car to go to the airfield. He went into the control tower to see Mr Satco, who was in charge of the airfield, and Mr Gale, the weatherman.

Mr Gale said that the weather would be all right for Jimmy to fly to the mountain that afternoon, and Mr Satco told him that the top of the mountain was flat so Jimmy would be able to land Swifty up there.

The next thing for Jimmy to do was to get a pair of skis for Swifty, so he got back into his red car and off he went to see Mr Plank at the hardware shop. "Good morning, Jimmy" said Mr Plank cheerfully. "What can I do for you?"

"Good morning, Mr Plank," replied Jimmy. "I am going to fly up on to Blue Mountain to rescue those Boy Scouts, but I have to put some skis under Swifty's wheels so that I can land on the snow. Have you got a nice big pair of them?"

"You are in luck Jimmy," said the jolly shopkeeper. "I have one pair left. They are too big for anyone in Redville so they should be just right for Swifty."

And they were just right. Jimmy went back to the airfield and with the help of his Daddy's mechanics the skis were fixed to Swifty's wheels.

Swifty was delighted with them and when he heard that the boys were trapped up the mountain he said, "Come on then Jimmy, let's get off quickly and rescue them so that they can go to the Christmas party tomorrow."

Jimmy jumped into Swifty's cabin and with a roar from the engine, off they climbed towards Blue Mountain. It was quite a long flight and as they began to climb higher and higher to get to the top of the mountain, they could see the snow on the top, making it look just like a cake with some icing on it.

Jimmy landed the little aeroplane on the top of the mountain and all the boys rushed up to him to thank him for coming to rescue them. Swifty couldn't get all the boys and their tents into his cabin, so they had to split into two groups. The first group got in, with some of their equipment and with a roar from the engine, they sped across the snow and zoomed up into the air.

When Jimmy landed Swifty back at the airfield, there was a large crowd of people waiting there for them. The Boy Scouts unloaded their equipment and Jimmy gave them a wave and took off again for Blue Mountain in order to bring the rest of the Scouts and their equipment back to Redville Airfield.

All the boys' Mummies and Daddies were there, together with the Lord Mayor, Mr Trundle. They were so pleased to see the children safely back and everyone said a big "Thank you" to Jimmy and Swifty.

They were very brave and clever to fit the skis and fly up into the mountain to rescue the boys, weren't they?

4

The Snow Models

Jimmy jumped out of bed one Monday morning, hoping that the snow would be just as thick on the ground as it had been the day before.

Mr Trundle the Mayor had announced that if it was still thick on the ground, he would hold a competition to see who could make the best snow model.

Jimmy loved playing in the snow, and he was very clever at making models, so he hoped that he would win the prize.

The competition didn't start until ten o'clock, so Jimmy got out his red car and drove down to the airfield to make sure that Swifty was all right.

"Hello Swifty," he called. "How are you today?"

"I'm very well, thank you, Jimmy," the magic aeroplane replied. "Are we going flying?"

"No, not today," said the little boy. "I am going to make a snow model for a competition. The only trouble is that I don't quite know what to make. Have you any ideas?"

Swifty thought and thought and then he said, "Why don't you make a model of me?"

Jimmy thought that it was a splendid idea, and after saying goodbye to the aeroplane, he got into his car again and went back to the field behind his Mummy's house, where the competition was to be held.

All the children were there, waiting for the Mayor to arrive. PC Crump had marked out a piece of snow-covered ground for each of the children and had put a card in front of each place with the name of the particular boy or girl on it.

The Mayor drove up in his official car, wearing the gold chain of office round his neck. He had an enormous topcoat on, because although it was a sunny day, it was very cold. He made a short speech and then the competition began.

Jimmy took his little spade and started to pile the snow up into a long mound in the centre of his piece of ground. Then he started patting it into shape. In about ten minutes, he had made the long mound look just like Swifty's fuselage, which is the body of the aeroplane where the pilot and passengers sit. Then he started on the wings, which were the most difficult things to do because there are of course two of them and they have to be exactly the same or they just won't look right.

Jimmy had a rest and looked up to see how the other children were doing with their models.

Johnny Green was making a model of a car; Bully Bloggs a ship and Lucy Lubbit a model house. They all looked very good.

Jimmy got back to work and soon had the tail finished. He looked at the model carefully and it was just like Swifty, but there were no decorations on it so he went round looking for some. Five minutes later he was back with his arms full of assorted objects.

He dumped the pile on the ground and picked out a piece of wood. He put this on the front of the fuselage so that it looked just like a propeller, and then he used some leaves and small sticks to finish the job of decorating the model.

Peep! The Mayor's whistle blew at that moment and all the children stopped work.

Mr Trundle and the policeman walked slowly round the field for about twenty minutes, then the Mayor gathered the children round to give his decision.

"I have been very impressed with your work, children," he said. "In fact, the models were so good that I am not going to award a prize to anyone. Instead, I am going to have a party for you all at the Town Hall this afternoon and I want you all to come."

The children clapped and cheered, and that afternoon they all turned up at the Town Hall, where they had one of the nicest parties they had ever had. They all hoped it wouldn't be too long before there was another snow model competition in Redville.

5

PC Crump Gets a Ducking

Jimmy woke up one morning feeling very excited.

The evening before, his father had brought home a box containing something which Jimmy had been wanting for a long time.

Can you guess what it was?

It was a pair of ice skates. The weather had been very cold for a week or two now so the day before, Jimmy had said to his father, "Daddy, you remember that you promised to buy me a pair of ice skates when the weather was cold enough? Well, the ice on the river is quite thick now, so do you think I could have a pair now, please?"

His Daddy said that on his way home from work that evening, he would see if he could find a pair in one of the shops. He was lucky, and Jimmy was delighted. He put them on, and they fitted perfectly.

Jimmy dressed and went down to breakfast, and as soon as he had finished eating, he put his warm clothes on, kissed his Mummy goodbye, picked up his new skates and dashed out of the house to get out his red car. He put his shiny new skates on the seat beside him and then off he went through Redville and out towards the river. He drove very carefully because there was a lot of ice on the roads, and at last he pulled up at the bank of the river where a number of children were already having a wonderful time on their skates.

Jimmy got out of the car and put on his new skates. He was so proud of them.

He stood up, tiptoed towards the river and stood on the ice. *Zap!* Over he went, falling flat on his back. This was the first time that Jimmy had ever been skating and he didn't know that at first it is very difficult to skate. He got up and tried again, and this time he managed to stay on his feet for a whole two minutes before falling flat on his back again. He tried again, time after time until at last he discovered how to skate properly.

He didn't fall down after that, and he had a lovely time. He whizzed up and down the river, then he made big circles on the ice with the marks from his skates and played tag with his friends.

All of a sudden, he noticed that his friends were laughing and pointing. He looked to where they were pointing and to his surprise, he saw PC Crump stepping gingerly on to the ice. The fat old policeman used to do a lot of skating in his younger days and when he saw the ice on the river, he couldn't resist the urge to get out his old skates.

He glided slowly out over the ice with a big smile on his face, but oh dear! Although the ice was quite thick enough to take the weight of the children, it wasn't nearly strong enough to take the policeman's weight and with a loud *Splosh!* he fell through the ice and into the water! He held on to the edge to keep his head above water and shouted, "Help!"

Jimmy skated across to where the poor policeman was shivering in the water.

"Give me your hand Constable Crump and I'll pull you out," he said. "It won't work Jimmy," replied the shivering policeman, "you just aren't strong enough."

So then Jimmy skated quickly over to his red car and got a rope out of the boot, tied one end of it to the bumper, threw the other to the policeman, started up the engine and slowly pulled him out of the water.

He got a blanket from the back seat and wrapped it round Constable Crump, then, driving as fast as he could, he took the policeman home.

By the time he had finished a nice hot bath, Jimmy had made him a nice cup of tea and got out the aspirins.

PC Crump was very grateful to Jimmy, and he said as much before he went upstairs to get into bed. Jimmy said he was happy to have helped him and then, closing the door behind him, he went off again to have some more fun on the ice with his friends.

6

Johnny Green's Christmas Present

It was Christmas Eve and Jimmy was fast asleep dreaming about the toys which he hoped would be on the bottom of his bed when he woke up in the morning.

Suddenly he woke up with a start.

Somebody was tapping on the window.

Can you guess who it was?

It was Santa Claus!   Jimmy dashed to the window and opened it.

"Hello," said Santa Claus, "you must be Jimmy. Can you help me? I have forgotten to bring Little Johnny Green's toys with me and if I go back all the way to my toy factory now my reindeer will be too tired to carry on with the job of delivering the toys to all the other children."

"Of course I shall help you," replied Jimmy. "There is a full moon tonight so I shall be able to see where Swifty and I are going. Now where is your toy factory?"

Santa told him about the secret toy factory and Jimmy was astonished! It was hidden in the wood behind Mr Barley's mill! Santa told him that he had a lot of toy factories all over the world and if you know where they are, and if you are very good, and if you say the secret word, you can get inside.

Jimmy had always thought that Santa's toy factory was at the North Pole, and he couldn't believe that one of the factories was not too far away. He got out his red car and drove quickly down to the airfield.

With a roar from Swifty's engine, off they went into the air and before long they had landed at the back of Mr Barley's mill. Jimmy dashed into the wood and knocked on the trunk of the old oak tree that Santa had told him about, at the same time saying, "Uggypopalop!"

A little gnome in a red costume invited Jimmy inside and the little boy gasped when he saw all the gnomes making lots and lots of toys.

"We have finished the toys for this year," said the little man. "We are making next year's now."

Jimmy told him about little Johnny Green's toys, which were soon found, and very few minutes later Jimmy and Swifty were on their way back to Redville with a bulging bag full of toys.

Santa was still waiting in the field at the back of Jimmy's house and he was very grateful when he saw the bag.

Because Jimmy and Swifty had been so kind he gave both of them both an extra special present each, a watch with luminous hands for Jimmy and a set of very bright lights to be fitted to Swifty's undercarriage to make it easier to land in the dark.

7
Twelfth Night

It was Twelfth Night in Redville.

Do you know what Twelfth Night is?

Well, it comes twelve days after Christmas Day and in the evening, all the people in Redville take down their Christmas decorations. I expect that it will happen in your house too.

They save their best ones for the next year but the paper chains and shiny tinsel are usually thrown away. Jimmy and his friends thought it a great pity to throw away such a large number of beautiful decorations so this year they had decided to take all the paper chains and tinsel up the hill behind the church.

At the top of the hill was a tree. It was a beautiful tree which always looked rather sad because it had no other trees close by.

Well, this year things were going to be different. The tree was going to have the time of its life!

Jimmy and his friends gathered together in the town square, their arms full of paper chains and long lengths of shiny tinsel. Somebody had even brought a very pretty fairy to put at the very top of the tree.

The children climbed up the path past the church and stopped at the little tree. They soon got to work and in no time, it began to look very pretty. Then Johnny Green had a bright idea.

"Why don't we light a big fire and roast some potatoes when we have finished the decorating?" he said, and they all thought it was a great idea. Johnny went back down the hill to get a box of matches and some potatoes while some of the children went looking for dead wood for the fire.

Jimmy stayed at the tree to supervise the hanging of the paper chains and in about half an hour, the job was finished but for one thing. They couldn't climb high enough to put the fairy at the top of the tree.

Jimmy thought and thought about how to solve the problem and then he had an idea. He took the fairy and a bag of silver stars and went back down the hill to where his red car was parked. He jumped in and a few minutes later, he was at the airfield.

"Hello Swifty!" he called. "We are going to put a fairy on the top of a very special tree. I have made a big loop of string for the fairy to hang on to and we are going to drop it from the air."

"Ooh, lovely," replied the magic aeroplane. "I feel like a bit of exercise."

Jimmy jumped into Swifty's cabin, and they were soon on their way to the hill above the church.

Jimmy flew Swifty quite slowly and gently lower and lower and then headed towards the tree. At just the right moment he let go of the fairy and the loop fell right onto the highest branch.

Jimmy and Swifty then flew higher and higher in a circle to a point where he emptied the bag of silver stars out over the hill.

It made a really lovely scene with the tree all sparkling and pretty coloured in the light from the bonfire and the stars floating down like big snowflakes.

Jimmy flew Swifty back to the airfield and after saying a big thank you and goodnight, he went back to the bonfire.

A lot of the Redville folk had gone up the hill to see the tree. They all thought it looked very beautiful, and Mr Chop the butcher had brought a basket of sausages, bacon, liver and an enormous frying pan. They cooked the meat and the potatoes and had a lovely feast, then as it was getting a little late, they said goodnight to the tree and went happily back down the hill.

That was a very nice way to celebrate Twelfth Night, wasn't it?

The next morning Jimmy and his friends went back to the tree to clear up because they didn't want the decorations to blow all over the fields and make a mess.

It was a beautiful morning with a clear blue sky and not a breath of wind anywhere.

"It's a pity that the fairy and all these pretty stars will have to go in the dustbin," said Jimmy, and then a strange thing happened. From nowhere a gentle breeze sprang up and the branches of the tree began to whisper as it passed through them.

Then, to their astonishment, the stars which had fallen on the ground lifted off the grass and began to float on the breeze.

They didn't fly away though. They circled the tree, climbing higher and higher and as they climbed, the decorations which were on the tree gently detached themselves and joined in the procession until the fairy at the top of the tree was the only thing left.

The stars hung there for a moment providing a sparkling carpet for her and then she too rose into the air and was carried away on her carpet of stars.

Do you know, the fairy and her magic stars were never seen again.

I wonder where they went?

8

That Naughty Bully Bloggs

Jimmy Robinson and Swifty the magic aeroplane were flying back to Redville one day when they saw little Johnny Green sitting at the side of the road crying.

"Shall we land and see what's the matter?" said Swifty. "He does look very sad."

Jimmy landed Swifty in a field at the side of the road and he got out to ask Johnny what was the matter.

"Oh, Jimmy," Johnny sobbed, "I was taking my little puppy Spot for a walk when Bully Bloggs came up and took Spot away from me. Please help me to get him back."

"Swifty and I will soon get him back for you," said Jimmy. "Jump in and we'll go and find Bully Bloggs."

Off they went into the sky and Jimmy set course for Cherry Tree Farm. Swifty landed beside the big white farmhouse and when Mrs Merry came out they told her about what Bully Bloggs had done and asked her if she had seen the naughty boy.

"I haven't seen him today," she answered. "But I know who will help you.   Police Constable Crump is inside the farmhouse having a cup of tea. Why don't we ask him?"

PC Crump was a very kind policeman as all policemen are but when he heard about Bully Bloggs, he became very stern. He told them that he had not seen the naughty boy but that he would help them to look for him.

He jumped in beside Jimmy and Johnny and off they went again. They soon saw Mr Stamp the postman who was riding from farm to farm delivering letters. Swifty landed in a field beside the postman and PC Crump asked him if he had seen Bully.

"Yes, I have seen him," said the postman. "He was walking down the road towards the red windmill. Can I help you to find him?"

In jumped Mr Stamp and off they went. They flew along the road and over Oak Wood, and finally landed on the road beside the red windmill. Mr Barley the miller was there to meet them.

"Are you looking for Bully Bloggs?" he asked.

"Yes," they chorused. "He has stolen Johnny's puppy, Spot."

The jolly miller said that when he had asked Bully what he was doing with Johnny's puppy, the naughty boy had run off into Oak Wood.

They left Swifty beside the windmill and Jimmy, Johnny, Mr Stamp, PC Crump and Mr Barley raced off in the direction of the wood. They searched through the trees looking for the boy and the puppy, but they couldn't find them anywhere.

Then Mr Barley remembered that there was a cave hidden in the wood, so they all crept quietly up to the cave entrance and PC Crump went inside. He soon came out again with Bully Bloggs held in one hand and the little puppy in the other.

"You naughty boy," said PC Crump sternly. "I am going to take you home and tell your parents what you have been up to."

They all climbed into Swifty's cabin, and the magic aeroplane took Mr Stamp back to where he had left his bicycle. Jimmy and Swifty then took the rest of the party back to Redville where PC Crump marched off to take Bully Bloggs home.

"I am so happy now that I have got my little puppy Spot back," said Johnny. "Thank you very much, Jimmy and Swifty, for helping me to find him. You must come with me, Jimmy, and have tea at my house."

Jimmy said goodnight to Swifty and then the two boys and the puppy jumped into Jimmy's red car and off they went to Johnny's house for a lovely tea.

9

Jimmy Helps the Campers

Jimmy was flying along in Swifty the aeroplane one day when they saw a group of children standing beside a bus and looking very sad.

"Shall we drop in and see what's the matter, Jimmy?" asked Swifty.

"Yes, I think that we had better see if we can help them," replied Jimmy.

He flew Swifty round and round in a circle, lower and lower and finally landed in a field beside the road. Jimmy got out of Swifty's cabin and went to ask the children what the problem was.

Johnny Green was with the children and he told Jimmy what had happened.

"We are very upset, Jimmy," he said. "We are going to take our tents and some food and live in a field at Mrs Merry's farm for a few days. The bus broke down when we got this far and the driver has gone to get his tools to mend it, but it will be dark before we reach Mrs Merry's farm and we won't be able to see to put the tents up."

"Oh dear," said Jimmy, "that is a pity. I wonder if there is anything that I can do to help."

Jimmy is a very kind little boy and he likes to help people when he can.

He walked over to Swifty and told him about the problem.

"The children are very sad, Swifty. They are going to live in tents at Mrs Merry's farm for a few days but their bus has broken down so it will be dark if they don't get there soon. I wish that we could help them."

"Well, we can," replied Swifty "We could take just a few children and some tents to Mrs Merry's farm ourselves and then while they are putting the tents up, we can come back for the rest of them together with their food."

Wasn't that a good idea?

Jimmy thought so too, and he went back to tell Johnny Green and his friends the news.

"Oh, that is a great idea," said Johnny breaking into a big, happy smile.

"Right then, we shall take three boys first together with the tents and they can start putting the tents up while we go and fetch the rest of the boys and the food."

They piled the tents into the cabin and then three boys climbed in and strapped themselves into their seats. With a roar from his engine, Swifty whizzed across the field and into the air. Over the river they went and across Oak Wood. They all waved to Mr Barley as they passed over his mill and at last, they arrived at Mrs Merry's farm.

Mrs Merry was there to meet them. "I am so pleased to see you, children," she smiled, "but I thought you were coming in the bus."

They told her what had happened, and she said that as it could be dark before they put their tents up she would make them a quick cup of tea so that they could get on with the job.

The boys all said, "Hooray!" and Jimmy and Swifty went back to pick up the rest of the children and the food before roaring back into the air on the way to Mrs Merry's farm. They had left a note to the bus driver to tell him what they had done so that he wouldn't be worried about where the boys were.

Over the river and Oak Wood they flew, waving to Mr Barley the miller again as they passed over his flour mill and were soon landing back at Mrs Merry's farm where they were delighted to find that the tents had already been erected.

It was starting to get dark, so Mrs Merry told them that to save time she would be happy to make them a special tea in the farmhouse.

They had a lovely party, with lots of tea, bread, home-made jam and fresh cream cakes.

When they were all full up, Jimmy said that he and Swifty had better be off before it got really dark.

"Thank you very much Jimmy," said Johnny Green. "If you and Swifty hadn't been there to help us, I don't know what would have happened."

Jimmy said goodnight to all the boys and then he and Swifty took off for their flight back to Redville.

Wasn't he a kind little boy?

10

A Fire in the Woods

Jimmy was sitting at home one day when the telephone rang. It was Mr Sparks, the head fireman from the fire station.

"Hello Jimmy," he said, "I wonder if you can help me. There is a fire in the woods behind Mr Barley's flour mill and it is too far off the road for my fire engines to reach it. We have some special powder which we can drop onto the fire to put it out but it needs to be dropped from an aeroplane. The aeroplane we normally use is unserviceable so I was wondering if you and Swifty could do the job for me."

Jimmy remembered that Santa Claus had a secret toy factory in the wood, so he immediately said, "Yes of course we'll be able to help you, Mr Sparks. I shall be at the airfield in ten minutes."

He put on his warm clothes and dashed out of the house to get out his red car and in no time at all, he was on his way to the airfield.

Swifty was waiting for him when he got there.

"Hello Jimmy," he said. "What's all the rush about?"

"The woods behind Mr Barley's mill are on fire, and we are going to drop some special powder onto the fire to put it out," replied the little boy.

Just at that moment Mr Sparks turned up in his car with some big boxes in the back. Jimmy helped him to load the boxes into Swifty's cabin and then with a roar from Swifty's engine, off they went into the air.

Swifty flew just as fast as he could, over the river and the fields, over the roads and the farmhouses and long before they reached the woods they could see the smoke coming up from the fire.

"Oh dear, Mr Sparks," said Jimmy, feeling very worried, "do you think that we shall be able to put the fire out with the amount of powder we have with us?"

"No, I don't Jimmy," replied the fireman, "we shall have to use this load and then go back for some more. Two loads should do the trick."

They eventually got to the fire and Jimmy flew low over the woods while Mr Sparks emptied the boxes out over the side of Swifty's cabin. Soon they were all empty. The fire had gone down a lot, but it was still moving to where Jimmy knew Santa's secret factory was.

He turned Swifty round and flew back to Redville as fast as the magic aeroplane could take them. He turned on the radio and made a call to Mr Satco at the airfield asking him to have some more powder ready, and sure enough, when they came to a stop beside Mr Satco's office there was another pile of boxes.

They loaded them up as fast as they could go and then they were back in the air again. Over the river and the fields they went, over the roads and the farms, until at last they arrived at the wood at the back of Mr Barley's flour mill.

Jimmy flew Swifty very low over the fire and once again Mr Sparks tipped the contents of the boxes over the side.

When all the boxes were empty, Jimmy circled over the woods to see if the fire had been put out, and to his delight he couldn't see a single wisp of smoke. The fire was out!

"Well done, Jimmy!" cried Mr Sparks. "You have done a wonderful job."

Jimmy breathed a huge sigh of relief. He was delighted to see that the fire had not got as far as Santa's secret toy factory. He couldn't tell Mr Sparks about the factory though as it was very, very secret.

They flew steadily back to Redville Airfield and when Mr Sparks had gone back to his office, Jimmy told Swifty that the magic aeroplane had saved the wood, Mr Barley's mill and Santa's secret toy factory.

A fantastic job!

11

An Airliner in Trouble

Jimmy was at the airfield one day giving Swifty a wash and brush up.
When Jimmy and Swifty had helped to put out the fire in the woods behind Mr Barley's mill the magic aeroplane had become covered in soot and smuts.

"Just one more wing to do, Swifty," called Jimmy, "and then you will look as good as new."

"Oh, thank you Jimmy," replied the magic aeroplane. "I feel a lot better already. Can we go and fly soon, it's such a lovely day?"

Jimmy was just about to reply when Mr Satco the airfield controller called from his office.

"Can you spare me a minute, Jimmy?"

"Certainly Mr Satco," replied the little boy, and then he said to the aeroplane, "Shan't be a minute, Swifty."

He walked across to Mr Satco's window.

"I wonder if you can help me, Jimmy," said the kind man. "There is a big jet airliner at Ivytown Airport, and his radio set is broken. They haven't got a spare set so they rang me up to see if we had one. The chief mechanic says that we can lend them one but I need someone to take it across there.

The airliner can't take off without it because the Captain won't be able to talk to the ground once it is in the air if he doesn't have a radio set."

"Certainly, I can help," said the little boy. "Just let me finish the job I am doing on Swifty and I'll be ready."

He went back and told the little aeroplane the news. Swifty was pleased because, as he had said, it was a lovely day for flying.

In ten minutes, the job was finished and with a big parcel behind him in the cabin, Jimmy took Swifty off into the air.

Over the fields and the farms they went, over the woods and the rivers until at last they came to the big airport at Ivytown. Jimmy landed gently and taxied to a stop beside the huge airliner. It was a jumbo jet and it looked enormous beside Swifty, as indeed it was.

Jimmy lifted the parcel out of the cabin and walked across to where the Captain of the airliner was waiting. He looked very smart in his blue uniform with four gold rings on his sleeve showing that he was the Captain. Captains of ships have the four gold rings on their sleeves too.

Jimmy put the parcel on the floor and shook hands with the man.

"I can't tell you how grateful I am," said the Captain. "My passengers want to go to Canada and some of them are in a hurry."

"Oh, that's a pleasure," replied the little boy. "We were going to fly anyway, so it was no trouble and I've never been close to an airliner before."

"Well, you must come and have a closer look," said the Captain. "Tell you what, I've got a better idea. We had to mend a part on one of our engines as well as changing the radio and I have to take off for a little while to make sure that it is working properly. Would you like to come?"

Jimmy was thrilled, and as soon as the radio man had put the new radio in and checked that it worked well, Jimmy and the crew climbed aboard. The airliner had a crew of four men and six lady Air Hostesses who were needed to look after all the passengers.

With a tremendous roar from the four engines, the airliner took off and climbed steeply. After a few minutes, the Captain levelled off and they flew round in a circle to check that the engine worked perfectly.

Twenty minutes later they were down on the ground again and after saying thank you to the Captain, Jimmy climbed down onto the tarmac. He waited to watch the passengers climb aboard and waved as the Captain took the huge airliner to the end of the runway and went off on his journey to Canada.

When the huge aircraft was only a small dot in the sky, Jimmy and Swifty took off and flew back to Redville.

Jimmy had had a very exciting day. Flying in the airliner had been a wonderful experience, but it was nice to fly in his own aeroplane again.

They landed back at Redville and after Jimmy had said goodnight to Swifty, he went off home in his red car to tell his Mummy and Daddy what an amazing adventure he had had.

12

Jimmy Remembers Meeting Swifty

Jimmy was sitting in his bedroom on a rainy and windy day when he found himself remembering how he had first met Swifty. Jimmy loved aeroplanes and his Daddy was the chief mechanic in the hangar at Redville Airfield. A hangar is a huge building where aeroplanes are stored while others are mended by the mechanics if they need it.

Jimmy remembered that day when he went into the hangar at lunchtime while the men were away and he heard crying from beneath a large tarpaulin in the corner. He was amazed to find that the crying was coming from a dirty old aeroplane. It's wings were on the ground; it had no propeller and its tyres were flat.

"Please help me," came a voice from the aeroplane. "I have been left here for such a long time and I would love to be able to fly again. If someone could mend me it would be wonderful."

When he got over his astonishment, Jimmy had asked Mr Satco the Airport Manager if he could have the aeroplane so that he could find out how these machines worked and the Manager had said that since no one wanted it, Jimmy could have it.

Over the next few weeks, Jimmy worked at the hangar when the men were away having their meals. He got the tyres pumped up using the pump from his red car. He used the hangar equipment to put the wings back on, and when he asked Mr Satco if he knew of anywhere where he could get a propeller, the manager said that the propeller which belonged to the aeroplane was in a shed at the back of the hangar, and that Jimmy was welcome to have it.

Jimmy used some more equipment to put the propeller on and then got to work cleaning and polishing the machine.

It was finished and as Jimmy stood back to admire his work, a voice came from the aeroplane.

"Thank you for doing such a lovely job. My name is Swifty and I am a magic aeroplane. I shall be very happy to teach you how to fly me if you would like me to."

"Well my name is Jimmy and Mr Satco says that since no one cares for you, you now belong to me."

That is how the friendship between the little boy and the aeroplane started.

They have already had some great adventures together and they are looking forward to having many more.

13
Swifty Goes for the Doctor

Jimmy was flying along with Swifty one day when down below he saw a little boy sitting at the side of the road, crying and holding his knee. It was Johnny Green. He had fallen off his bicycle and the front wheel was now broken, so he couldn't ride to the Doctor's house to get his knee bandaged up and his poorly knee meant that it was too far to walk.

Jimmy looked around for a place to land but there were trees everywhere so he asked Swifty what he thought they ought to do.

"Well, why don't we fly back to Redville and get Doctor Jones?" replied the magic aeroplane.

"Yes, that is a good idea, Swifty, but even if we go and fetch Doctor Jones we still can't land anywhere near poor Johnny."

Then Jimmy had an even better idea.

"I know what we can do, Swifty," he said, "we can fly back here with the Doctor and he can jump out using a parachute. There is a club of parachutists at Redville Airfield and I am sure they will lend one to him as it is an emergency.

You will remember what a parachute is when it was used to parachute food down to the miller and Mrs Merry.

Off went Jimmy and Swifty in the direction of Redville, over the farms and the fields they went, over the woods and the river until at last they landed at Redville Airfield.

As soon as they had landed, Jimmy dashed off to the control tower to Mr Satco's office and asked if he could use his telephone. Mr Satco said, "Certainly Jimmy," and in no time at all Jimmy was talking to Doctor Jones.

"Hello Doctor," he said. "Johnny Green has fallen off his bicycle and badly hurt his knee. His bicycle is broken so he can't get to you and he is a long way away in some woods in a small clearing, but there isn't enough room in the clearing for Swifty to land there. Is there a chance that you could borrow a parachute from the Parachute Club so that you could come with us and jump out to help him?"

"Yes, I will certainly help him," said the Doctor. "I am a member of the Parachute Club so I shall use my own parachute. I shall call the hospital and ask them to send an ambulance so that by the time I have patched up Johnny's knee the ambulance should be there. You show me where the clearing is on this map, and I'll tell them where to go to find him."

Within a few minutes, Doctor Jones' big shiny car drew up at the airfield and out got the Doctor with his medical bag full of bandages and medicines. Jimmy put the bag into Swifty's cabin while Doctor Jones collected his parachute, and they were soon back in the air.

Swifty flew as fast as he could, back over the river and the woods, over the farms and fields until they got to the place where Johnny Green was still sitting by the side of the road. Doctor Jones clipped on his parachute, and with his medical bag tied to his belt, he jumped out of the aeroplane.

Jimmy and Swifty flew round in circles so that they could see the Doctor float gently down to land right beside the boy. They saw him working on Johnny's leg and a little while later, the ambulance arrived. The men in the ambulance put Johnny's bicycle in the back and with the Doctor and Johnny safely inside they set off back to Redville.

Johnny's leg soon got better, and he went down to the airfield to say a big "Thank you" to Jimmy and Swifty.

It was a very lucky thing that Jimmy spotted him at the side of the road that day, wasn't it?

14

Swifty Delivers the Mail

One day Jimmy was walking along the street when he came upon Mr Stamp the postman who was looking very glum.

"Hello Mr Stamp," called Jimmy. "Why are you looking so sad on a lovely day like this?"

"Oh, hello Jimmy," replied the unhappy postman. "My bicycle has broken down and I have a lot of letters and parcels to deliver. I can walk around Redville delivering some of the mail but I have got parcels and letters for Mrs Merry and some of the other country folk, and they live too far away for me to walk there."

"Oh dear, I can see now why you are so sad," said Jimmy. "Are they important letters?"

"Yes, they are. Mrs Merry has been waiting for this parcel of wool for a week and she must get it today because Mr Merry's birthday comes soon, and she wants to knit him a nice new sweater," moaned Mr Stamp. "She will be so disappointed."

"Well don't you worry," said Jimmy cheerfully. "Swifty and I will deliver your mail to the country people for you."

The kind postman's face broke into a big smile. He was so delighted that he did a little dance right there in the street.

Wasn't he a funny old man?

Jimmy and Mr Stamp sorted through the large post bag and got out all the letters and parcels which were addressed to the country folk. There weren't very many of them and Jimmy told the postman he would soon have the job done.

He got into his red car and drove down to the airfield. He got out of the car and, with all the mail in a bag, he went over to Swifty, his magic aeroplane.

"Good morning Swifty," he called, "how are you today? We are going to deliver some mail to the country folk for Mr Stamp because his bicycle has broken down."

Swifty was very pleased because he likes to do good turns for people and in no time at all, they were climbing into the air to deliver the mail.

Mrs Merry's parcel of wool was the most important thing they had so Jimmy set off in the direction of Cherry Tree Farm. Mrs Merry was surprised to see them landing in the field in front of the pretty white farmhouse, but when she saw that Jimmy was carrying her important parcel, she was delighted.

"Oh, you are kind!" she said. "I thought the parcel would never come. Let's go into the farmhouse and have a cup of tea."

"That would be very nice, thank you but I have some other important mail to deliver so I can't stop now, Mrs Merry," replied Jimmy and he jumped back into Swifty's cabin and took off into the air again.

The next parcel was quite heavy because it was a piece of machinery for Mr Barley's flour mill. Mr Barley has a big machine which turns corn and wheat into flour for making bread, but one of the parts of the machine was getting old so he needed the spare piece that Jimmy was bringing.

"Oh, thank you Jimmy," he said, "that is very kind of you. Come into the mill and have a nice glass of lemonade."

"No thank you Mr Barley," smiled Jimmy, "I have some more important mail to deliver so I mustn't stop."

Off went Jimmy and Swifty again, over the fields and the woods, landing at all the houses and the farms and delivering the mail. At last, he finished the job and he and Swifty flew back to Redville Airfield where Mr Stamp was waiting for them. He was so grateful that he invited Jimmy to go and have tea with him that afternoon and so, after saying thank you and goodbye to Swifty, Jimmy and the postman got into the red car and set off home.

Jimmy was a good boy to deliver the mail for the postman, wasn't he?

Do you do jobs for your Mummy and Daddy too?

15

Swifty's Owner Returns

Jimmy was playing in the garden one day when his Mummy called him to the telephone. It was Mr Satco from the airfield and he sounded very worried.

"Hello Jimmy," he said gloomily. "Would you like to come down to my office. I've got some bad news for you I'm afraid and I don't want to tell you on the telephone."

Jimmy was quite upset. He thought that perhaps Swifty's engine had gone wrong or that something had crashed into the little aeroplane. He ran to the garage to get out his red car and he was soon on his way to the airfield.

When he got there, he ran straight to Mr Satco's office and knocked on the door.

"Come in," said the voice of the gentle airfield manager. Jimmy opened the door and went inside. Mr Satco looked worried. "Hello Jimmy, come in and sit down," he said kindly.

Jimmy found a small chair in the corner and sat down.

"What's the matter?" asked the little boy.

"Well, you remember that day a long time ago when you came and asked me if anyone owned Swifty? I said that you could have him because nobody wanted him. I'm very sorry to say that a man came yesterday who said that Swifty belonged to him and that he wanted him back. I asked him to prove that Swifty was his and he showed me a piece of paper which proved it, so I'm afraid that Swifty will have to go away with him."

Jimmy started to cry. Swifty wasn't just an aeroplane, as you know, he was a dear friend of Jimmy's too.

"But Swifty belongs to me," he said. "They can't take him away, can they?"

"I'm afraid that they can, Jimmy," replied Mr Satco. "I thought that Swifty's real owner would never come back and that Swifty was in such a poor state that he would never fly again. That's why I said that you could have him."

"Can I go and say goodbye to him?" asked the little boy through his tears.

"Of course you can, Jimmy, the man won't be coming for a little while yet."

With a heavy heart, Jimmy walked slowly down to the hangar where Swifty was and told his aeroplane the awful news.

"I shall never see you again, Swifty," he said. "There is a man coming soon who is your real owner and he is going to take you away."

To his surprise Swifty chuckled. "Don't you worry about that, Jimmy," he said. "He left me here in the hangar, all broken and dirty and never once did he come to see me. If he thinks he is going to take me away, he'll have to think again. Now dry your eyes and go and have a cup of tea while I deal with him."

Jimmy walked over to the restaurant feeling much better and wondering what Swifty was going to do. He sat looking out of the window and a little while later he saw a big, fierce-looking man stride over to the hangar.

Ten minutes later, Jimmy heard the sound of Swifty's engine, and the little aeroplane came out of the hangar with the man at the controls.

Just at that moment, Swifty started to cough and splutter and then, in a cloud of smoke, he came to a standstill and his engine stopped.

The man climbed out and called a mechanic. Together they had a good look at Swifty's engine and then the man got inside again, started it up and moved Swifty out to the end of the runway ready for take-off. With a roar from Swifty's engine they started to take off, but halfway along the runway, just after they got into the air, Swifty's engine spluttered and died again so that the aeroplane slammed back onto the runway.

The man stalked back to the hangar looking red-faced and furious.

"That aeroplane is dangerous!" he shouted at the mechanic. "The engine keeps stopping. I never want to see it again and you can put it on the scrapheap for all I care." With that, he went over to his car and disappeared in a cloud of dust.

Jimmy dashed over to where Swifty stood. "Are you all right Swifty?" he asked. "I saw you take off and then crash back onto the runway. The man got out and he said that he was never coming back and that you should be put on the scrapheap."

"I told you I would make sure that he didn't fly away with me," chuckled Swifty. "Now take me back to the hangar and tomorrow we'll go and fly to the seaside for the day."

And that is just what they did.

16

A Surprise for Jimmy

One day Jimmy was sitting at the window waiting for his Daddy to come home from his office when his Mummy came into the room. "I think your Daddy may have a surprise for you when he comes home today Jimmy," she said.

Jimmy's eyes lit up. "Oh, what will it be?" he asked.

"You just wait and see," she replied, and he turned back to the window to keep an eye open for his Daddy's car, feeling very excited.

At last, he saw the big shiny car come round the corner with his Daddy at the wheel, so he dashed to the front door and waited to see what the surprise would be.

His Daddy got out of the car carrying a large basket from which came the strangest noises.

"Hello Jimmy," he called. "Guess what I've got for you? Is it a cat, or a guinea pig, or a puppy? Which one would you rather have?"

"Ooh! I'd rather have a puppy," said the little boy.

"Well open the basket and see what I have brought for you," said his Daddy with a smile.

Jimmy took the basket inside the house and unfastened the straps which held the lid down.

What do you think he saw when he opened the lid?

It was the softest, cuddliest, friskiest, sweetest little puppy he had ever seen. Jimmy was delighted. He picked it up in his arms very gently and was rewarded by a very wet tongue which licked his nose and face and made it tickle.

"Oh, thank you Daddy," said the little boy. "It's just what I've always wanted, a puppy of my own. What's his name?"

"Well, the man at the shop said it was Crispin," replied his Daddy. "Do you like that, or should we call him another name?"

"Oh no, I think that's a very nice name," said Jimmy. "Crispin it is," and the puppy gave a happy little *Yip! Yip!* as if to say, "Yes, I like that name too."

Crispin jumped out of Jimmy's arms and ran up and down and round and round the room. Then Jimmy got out his rubber ball and rolled it towards the little bundle of fur. The puppy very cleverly stopped it with his nose and nudged it back towards Jimmy, but before the little boy could get hold of it, Crispin ran after it and nudged it away again.

Jimmy and the puppy chased round the room, Crispin after the ball and Jimmy after Crispin. They had such a lot of fun.

Then Jimmy had a thought, and he said to his Daddy, "I do hope that Swifty will like Crispin, he's such a nice little puppy. Can I take him to the airfield so that he can meet him?"

"All right, Jimmy," said his father. "But don't be long, it's nearly time for your bath."

Jimmy popped Crispin into the red car and drove off to the airfield where Swifty was standing just outside the hangar.

"Hello Swifty!" called Jimmy.

"Hello Jimmy," replied the magic aeroplane. "What have you got there?"

"I'll show you" said the happy little boy and he took Crispin out of the car.

Well!

Crispin started to bark furiously. You see, he had never seen an aeroplane before, and it rather frightened him.

"Oh! What a noisy little thing," said Swifty. "I don't think I'm going to like him if he is going to make a noise like that all the time."

Crispin growled again and then, when he saw that Swifty wasn't a monster, he wagged his tail and went up to the aeroplane, giving a funny little *Yip! Yip! Yip!* sound, as if to say, "I've had my growl, shall we be friends now?"

Do you know, Swifty and Crispin became the very best of friends, and I'll tell you how it came about.

17

Swifty Makes Friends with Crispin

Jimmy and Crispin were getting along very well. Crispin loved to have the little boy throw the rubber ball across the garden so that he could chase after it and bring it back to Jimmy to do it again and again.

Jimmy's Daddy had bought a basket for the puppy to sleep in at the bottom of the little boy's bed, and he had his own blue dishes, one for his meat and biscuits and the other for his water.

Jimmy, however, was still a bit upset that Swifty hadn't taken to Crispin, so a few mornings after the puppy arrived, Jimmy took him down to the airfield again. When they got there, he stopped the car, picked up Crispin and went over to where Swifty was standing.

"Hello Swifty," he said. "How are you today?"

"Morning Jimmy," replied the magic aeroplane. "I'm very well, thank you. I see you've brought that noisy little puppy with you again. Can't you leave him in the car? I don't much like the way he barks."

"Oh, don't be like that Swifty," replied Jimmy. "He's really a very nice little puppy and although he makes a lot of noise, he's a very friendly fellow."

"He probably is, but I don't like the noise he makes," retorted the aeroplane "So please leave him in the car."

"Swifty! You're jealous!" said the little boy crossly. "Now don't be silly. Let's go and fly and when we land again, I want you to be nice to Crispin."

"Well, I don't know," said Swifty, "let's get into the air and then we'll see."

Jimmy went back to his red car and told Crispin to stay there while he and Swifty went flying. The puppy wasn't at all pleased, but after a couple of *raff-raffs*, he wagged his tail and sat on his seat. Jimmy wound the window down a little bit so that Crispin would have some fresh air in the car and the little puppy watched him walk back towards Swifty.

Jimmy hadn't gone very far, however, before the little puppy jumped out of the car and chased after him. Jimmy picked him up and walked back to the car.

"Now you be a good little puppy and stay there," he said, then off he went again towards the aeroplane. Once more he hadn't gone very far before Crispin was at his feet. Jimmy picked him up again. "Now look, Crispin," he said sternly, "if you want Swifty to like you, you'd better stay here and wait while we go and fly."

The little puppy stayed there this time with his back paws on the seat and his front paws on the window ledge, wagging his tail even harder.

"Come on then Swifty," said Jimmy when he reached the aeroplane. "Let's go and have a quick trip and then you can make friends with Crispin."

He pressed the button which started Swifty's engine, and they started to taxi across the tarmac. Suddenly Swifty stopped.

"Jimmy," he said, "just look where your naughty little animal is now. I thought that you were going to leave him in the car."

"Well, I did," said Jimmy. "Where is he now?"

He looked out of the cabin and there, right in front of Swifty's wheels, was Crispin.

"Out of my way please, Crispin!" shouted Jimmy over the sound of Swifty's engine, but the little puppy just stayed there, wagging his tail and barking.

"Now come on, Crispin!" shouted Jimmy sternly. "We want to fly, so don't be silly, get out of the way."

The little puppy just looked back, saying,` "Raf! Raf! Raf! Raf!" and stayed just where he was without moving.

"Oh dear, Swifty," said Jimmy, "I'll have to get out and take him back to the car. I won't be long."

He climbed down and walked towards the little dog, then he saw why Crispin was barking. Right on the ground in front of Swifty's wheels, one of the mechanics had accidentally dropped a bunch of nails and if the clever little puppy hadn't stopped them, Swifty would have run over the nails and both of his tyres would have burst.

When Jimmy told Swifty what Crispin had done, the little aeroplane was ashamed of himself.

"I'm very sorry, Crispin, for being so rude," he said. "If you don't mind, I'd like to be friends now".

The puppy *Yip! Yip! Yipped* and wagged his tail till Jimmy thought it would fall off.

Swifty said, "Jimmy, put Crispin in my cabin and let's all go for a flight."

And that's what they did. Crispin sat on the other front seat with his feet on the windowsill, watching the world go by and wagging his tail.

18

Jimmy Goes Crop Spraying

Jimmy was flying along one day in Swifty when, looking down, he saw Mrs Merry standing beside one of her fields looking most upset.

"Mrs Merry doesn't look very pleased, Swifty," said the little boy. "I wonder what's the matter."

"Well, let's go and find out; I've got plenty of petrol left in my tank," replied the little aeroplane.

They swooped down and landed in the field next to where the farmer's wife was standing.

"Hello Mrs Merry," called Jimmy. "Is something wrong?"

"Hello Jimmy," she said sadly. "Yes, it's my potato crop. It was perfectly all right last week but it is covered with insects now. They are starting to eat the leaves and I don't know how I am going to get rid of them."
"Well, can't you spray the plants with stuff to get rid of the insects?" asked Jimmy.

"Yes, I could try, but the field is so enormous it would take me weeks to cover it and by that time all the plants would be eaten up," replied the lady.

Just at that moment, Swifty's engine gave a little cough, which meant that the magic aeroplane wanted to talk to Jimmy, so the little boy excused himself and went over.

"I know how we can get rid of those greedy insects, Jimmy," said Swifty. "We used to have some men at Redville Airfield who had special equipment fitted to their aeroplanes. They used to fill the boxes with powder and then fly over the fields, spreading it all over the crops. Sometimes it was food for the plants, but mostly it was special powder to get rid of insects which were damaging the crops."

"That's all very well, Swifty," said Jimmy, "but they aren't there now, so how can we help?"

"Well, they sold their aeroplanes to a man from Ivytown but the new owner didn't want the boxes and pipes so they were left at Redville and as far as I know, they are still there."

Jimmy rushed back to Mrs Merry and told her that they might be able to help her, then he jumped into Swifty's cabin, and they roared off into the air.

When they arrived at Redville, Jimmy went straight to see Mr Satco and asked him if the powder boxes and the pipes were still there, and to his delight the Airfield Manager said that they were, and that Jimmy could borrow them.

The little boy went to see the mechanics next and told them about Mrs Merry's problem. The kind men were only too ready to help, and they worked all through their lunch hour to fit the equipment to Swifty.

While they were doing this, Jimmy went and bought several boxes of insect powder from the farm supplies store. Mrs Merry had already agreed to pay the store for the powder. He then put the boxes into his red car and drove back to the airfield where the mechanics had just finished the job.

They filled the boxes with powder and took off for Mrs Merry's farm. As soon as they got there, Jimmy flew Swifty over the potato field and pressed the switch to gradually release the powder.

When the field was covered with it, they returned to Redville and Jimmy got on the telephone to Mrs Merry to tell her what they had done. She was very grateful, and the next morning she rang Jimmy to tell him that the insects didn't like the powder at all, and they had all disappeared! Her potato crop was looking very healthy again.

The mechanics removed the crop-spraying equipment from Swifty, and Jimmy gave him a polish so that he looked like new again.

It was clever of Swifty to remember about the crop-spraying aeroplanes, wasn't it?

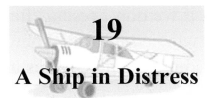

19

A Ship in Distress

Jimmy was sitting at home listening to the radio one day. The weather outside was awful; it was pouring down with rain and the wind whistled through the trees at the bottom of the garden.

The newsreader on the radio was saying that a ship was caught on the rocks in the storm, just outside Seatown, and the crew were in great danger.

Just then a knock came at the door and Jimmy's Mummy went to answer it.

It was PC Crump. Jimmy's Mummy invited him in and called Jimmy to the sitting room.

"Hello Jimmy," said the policeman. "I don't know whether or not you would be prepared to help, but you may have heard on the news that there is a ship in great danger just outside Seatown. We need someone to get a get a rescue line out to the men on the ship and the wind is too strong for our rescue rockets. The rope could be dropped from an aeroplane but it would be very dangerous, so if you say that you would rather not do it, I shall understand."

Jimmy looked at his Mummy.

"Please may I go Mummy?" he asked. "I shall be quite safe with Swifty and those men will drown if we don't rescue them soon."

His Mummy was very worried, but she knew that if anyone could save those sailors it would be Jimmy and Swifty so, reluctantly, she said that he could go.

Jimmy put on his waterproof clothes and dashed out to his red car. Crispin ran out after him, but Jimmy said, "No, not this time Crispin, it's far too dangerous for a puppy," and he handed the little fellow back to his Mummy.

Jimmy started the car, switched on the headlights and the windscreen wipers, then he and PC Crump drove off towards the airfield.

Swifty was surprised to see them.

"Hello Jimmy," he called. "You surely don't want to go flying on a day like this, do you?"

"No, we don't," replied the little boy, "but I'm afraid we've got to. You see, there are some sailors in a ship which has been driven onto the rocks by the storm and if we don't fly over and drop a rescue line to them, they will all drown. It's going to be very difficult, Swifty. We shall have to land on the clifftop to pick up the line. Then we must take off again with one end of the line, fly over the ship and drop it to the sailors. Do you think we shall be able to manage it?"

"Well we'll have a jolly good try," replied the magic aeroplane. "I'm ready if you are."

Jimmy and the policeman climbed into Swifty's cabin and the little boy switched on the radio. "Hello, Mr Satco," he called. "Can you hear me?"

"Yes Jimmy. I can hear you. Are you ready to go?"

"All set, but can you switch on the runway lights please? The rain is very heavy, and we shan't be able to see very well for take-off if we don't have them."

"OK Jimmy" replied the Airfield Manager, and the lights on each side of the runway came on.

"Here we go then, Constable Crump," said Jimmy, and they taxied out to the end of the runway.

He lined Swifty up exactly on the centre line of the runway then, telling the policeman to hold on tight he opened the throttle and roared down the tarmac into the air.

The wind bumped and jostled them, and the rain battered at Swifty's windscreen. Jimmy circled the airfield until he saw the silver ribbon of the river below, then he followed it down towards the coast.

They bounced on through the storm and finally they saw the houses of Seatown below. They flew over the town until they got to the sea, and then they turned and flew along the cliffs.

After about five minutes they saw the huge ship. It was jammed on the rocks and the waves were breaking right over the top of it. Jimmy and the policeman looked hard and saw the small group of men standing on the clifftop.

"Do you think we shall be able to land there, Jimmy?" asked the very worried policeman. "It looks a very small landing ground."

"If this were an ordinary aeroplane, I'm sure we wouldn't be able to make it, but this is Swifty and if he says that we can do it, then I'm sure we can. What do you think, Swifty?"

"Well, it won't be easy, Jimmy," replied the magic aeroplane, "but I think we'll manage it, and my landing lights will help us to see ahead as we come in to land. Strap yourselves in tight in case one of my wheels hits a rock on landing. Are we ready?"

Jimmy turned the aeroplane and flew lower and lower through the bumpy air and the rain until finally they flashed over a hedge and bumped down onto the grass.

They were down.

"Well done, Swifty!" cried Jimmy.

"I couldn't have done it without your help," replied the little aeroplane. "That was the most difficult landing I have ever had to make, but the hardest part of this job is going to be taking off from here with the rope and dropping it to the ship. I don't know whether or not we shall be able to do it."

In the next chapter I'll tell you how they managed to rescue the sailors and took one of them to the hospital.

20

A Ship in Distress, The Rescue

D o you remember that there was a ship caught on the rocks outside Seatown in a bad storm, and how the sailors on the ship were in great danger, and how Jimmy and PC Crump in Swifty landed on the clifftop to pick up a rescue line to take over to the ship? Well, Swifty wasn't sure whether or not they would be able to do the job of taking the line out to the sailors in trouble.

The men on the clifftop waited until Swifty had come to a stop and then they ran over to congratulate Jimmy on the landing he had made.

"Thank you for coming, Jimmy," said the Coastguard. "We fired our rockets with the lines attached but the wind blew them away and we only have one line left so we can't afford to make a mistake this time. Do you think you can do the job?"

"To be honest, I don't know," replied the little boy truthfully. "I'll have to get out and measure the landing field to see if there is enough room for me to take off, then I'll be able to tell you."

Jimmy got out of Swifty's cabin and walked all over the clifftop, inspecting the surface of the ground and asking the men to move the odd rock out of the way. Finally, he went over to the magic aeroplane.

"Swifty, I think that with a bit of luck we shall be able to manage it. What do you think?"

"Well, I'm prepared to have a go, Jimmy," replied the aeroplane.

Jimmy walked back to the Coastguard and said, "I've decided to have a try. Will you get your men to coil up the line very carefully so that it runs out evenly?"

The Coastguard's men carried the line over to Swifty very carefully. They used a thin line to start with and this was joined to a thicker line which in turn was joined to an even thicker one. Swifty was going to drop the thin line to the ship, then the sailors would pull on it until they got the thickest line on board and once this heavy line had been secured to the ship it would make a bridge between the stricken ship and the clifftop.

At last, the line was all neatly stowed in Swifty's cabin. On Jimmy's instructions, the little aeroplane was pushed right back to the hedge so that they had the maximum take-off run. The men fastened one end of the line to a tree, then signalled to the little boy that they were ready.

The wind was really blowing hard, but that was a good thing because if an aeroplane takes off into a strong wind it doesn't need such a long runway.

Jimmy pressed the switch and Swifty's engine roared into life.

"Well, Constable Crump, are you ready?"

The policeman swallowed hard and nodded his head.

"Let's go then!" shouted the little boy over the noise of the storm and he pushed open the throttle as far as it would go. He kept the brakes on until the engine was going as fast as it could, then he let go and the aeroplane shot forward across the grass.

Nearer and nearer came the edge of the cliff, and for a moment Jimmy thought that they weren't going to make it, but just at the last second, Swifty's wheels came off the ground and they were airborne!

The wind bumped and jostled them, but Jimmy held a straight course and the line paid out smoothly behind them with the policeman making sure that it didn't catch on to anything. At last, they crossed over the ship and PC Crump threw out the weight which was attached to the end of the line.

Jimmy circled the ship and was delighted to see that the line landed right across it.

"Oh, well done Jimmy!" shouted the policeman. "Never thought you would manage it."

They flew round and round the ship, watching as the line grew thicker and thicker. Finally, the sailors were ready to be rescued, and Jimmy's delight turned to concern when he saw that the first of the sailors was being taken across on a special stretcher.

He turned to the policeman. "It will take hours to carry him across the fields and then there could be many trees down and blocking the roads to the hospital," he said. "There's only one thing to do."

"You mean land back on the clifftop and take him to hospital?" said Mr Crump, his face turning pale.

"Yes," replied the little boy. "I don't like the idea either, but he may be badly injured so we shall have to get him to a Doctor as fast as possible."

In the next chapter I'll tell you how Jimmy and Swifty made the most difficult take-off of their life to get the injured sailor to the hospital.

21

The Injured Sailor

Do you remember from our last chapter how Jimmy, Swifty and PC Crump flew out over the ship which was caught in a storm outside Seatown and how they dropped a rescue line to it? Then I told you that one of the sailors was injured and that Jimmy had decided to make another dangerous landing and take-off from the clifftop so that the man could be taken to hospital, as the roads were blocked by fallen trees.

The storm was still raging when Jimmy turned Swifty towards the clifftop for another landing. The wind bounced them around but Jimmy and Swifty fought hard and finally they bumped down onto the grass again.

The Coastguard ran over. "Thank heaven you've come back Jimmy," he puffed. "One of the sailors has a broken arm and a broken leg and you have obviously landed again to pick him up as the roads are blocked, and anyway, the nearest road is almost a mile over the fields, and we would have had to carry him."

"We'll take him to Redville Hospital," said the little boy, "but we shall need a longer take-off run with the weight of another man on board. We only just managed to take off last time."

The men puzzled over how best to provide Swifty with a longer run, and then they decided to pull out some of the hedge at the end of the field farthest away from the cliff edge so that Jimmy could use part of the field on the other side as well.

While the men were working, PC Crump, who was very good at first aid, had a good look at the injured sailor. Using the Coastguard's first aid box he put a splint on the man's leg and made a sling for his injured arm.

By the time the policeman had finished making him more comfortable the men had made a large gap in the hedge, and the rest of the sailors from the ship had been brought to safety on land, so they were able to help with the work of clearing the gap. They had all gone up to Jimmy and PC Crump and thanked them very sincerely for their bravery in flying during the dangerous storm to rescue them.

It was very hard work clearing a runway in the heavy rain and roaring wind. The men slipped and fell over on the wet grass and the rain soaked them through. To add to their troubles, it began to get dark!

Finally, the runway was ready, and Jimmy, PC Crump and the injured sailor were all in the cabin. The little boy had a last look round to make sure everything was as it should be and then he pressed the button to start Swifty's engine. With a roar it burst into life, and they were ready to go. Jimmy taxied Swifty through the gap in the hedge and into the field the other side. When they got to the middle of the field, they turned round, ready to take off again.

Although the men had made quite a wide gap in the hedge, it looked very small from where Jimmy was waiting to go, particularly since it was now almost dark. Jimmy switched on Swifty's landing lights to make things a bit clearer in the rain. He looked at the policeman who was sitting there, very nervous and with his eyes tightly shut!

"Well, just one more take-off and we'll be on our way home, Swifty," said Jimmy then he opened the throttle to increase the power of the engine, let go the brakes and Swifty shot forward over the grass. The gap in the hedge, which had seemed very small, now grew wider and wider as they approached it. They had a glimpse of the men standing by the gap and cheering as they went through and then they leapt into the air, well short of the edge of the cliff.

Jimmy turned Swifty towards Seatown and they climbed up through the storm. They flew along the coast until they saw the mouth of the river and turned to fly along it towards Redville.

Jimmy switched on the radio and called Mr Satco in the control tower "Hello Redville Airfield," he said, "this is Jimmy. I have an injured sailor on board, and I shall be landing in another ten minutes, so will you please switch on the landing lights and have an ambulance waiting?"

Almost immediately, far ahead, he saw the runway lights go on. The rain had stopped now and the clouds were beginning to go away, leaving a bright, moonlit view of the countryside.

Ten minutes later, they were on the ground, where they were met by an ambulance for the sailor and a whole crowd of Redville folk, including Mr Trundle, the Mayor.

Jimmy was so tired that he didn't want to stay chatting, and as soon as the sailor was safely on his way to the hospital he said goodnight and a big thank you to Swifty as he put him back in the hangar, then he politely wished all the people goodnight too, got into his red car and went home to bed for a well-earned rest, leaving Police Constable Crump to tell the story of his bravery that day.

BV - #0073 - 030322 - C11 - 210/210/4 - PB - 9781913839581 - Gloss Lamination